BODY WORKS™

MUSCLES
The Muscular System

Gillian Houghton

PowerKiDS press

New York

Published in 2007 by The Rosen Publishing Group, Inc.
29 East 21st Street, New York, NY 10010

First Edition

Editor: Amelie von Zumbusch
Book Design: Greg Tucker

Photo Credits: Cover, p. 5 © PASIEKA/Photo Researchers, Inc.; p. 6 (left) © Asa Thoresen/Photo Researchers, Inc.; p. 6 (right) © Professor Peter Cull/Photo Researchers, Inc.; pp. 9 (left), 21(right) © John M. Daugherty/Photo Researchers, Inc.; p. 9 (right) © David Pu'u/Corbis; p. 10 (left) © Don W. Fawcett/Photo Researchers, Inc.; p. 10 (right) © Reed Kaestner/Corbis; p. 13 © Birmingham/Custom Medical Stock Photo; p. 14 (left) © S. Gulka/zefa/Corbis; p. 14 (right) © Peter Beck/Corbis; p. 17 (left) © Michael A. Keller/zefa/Corbis; pp. 17 (right), 18 (right) © Articulate Graphics/Custom Medical Stock Photo; p. 18 (left) © Dan Kenyon/zefa/Corbis; p. 21 (left) © Ole Graf/zefa/Corbis.

Library of Congress Cataloging-in-Publication Data

Houghton, Gillian.
  Muscles : the muscular system / Gillian Houghton.— 1st ed.
      p. cm. — (Body works)
  Includes index.
  ISBN (10) 1-4042-3475-6 (13) 978-1-4042-3475-8 (lib. bdg.) — ISBN (10) 1-4042-2184-0 (13) 978-1-4042-2184-0 (pbk.)
  1. Muscles—Juvenile literature. I. Title. II. Series.
  QP321.H72 2007
  612.7'4—dc22
                              2006002753

Manufactured in the United States of America

Contents

The Muscular System ——————

Whether you are running a race or taking a nap, you are always using your muscles. Muscles are **tissues** that allow the body to move. The body's hundreds of different muscles make up the muscular system.

Some muscles control movements that take place inside the body. For example, muscles direct the movement of blood through the **circulatory system**. Muscles also control the movement of food through the **digestive system**. Other muscles control the movement of the body itself, such as the movement of your hand when you turn the pages of this book.

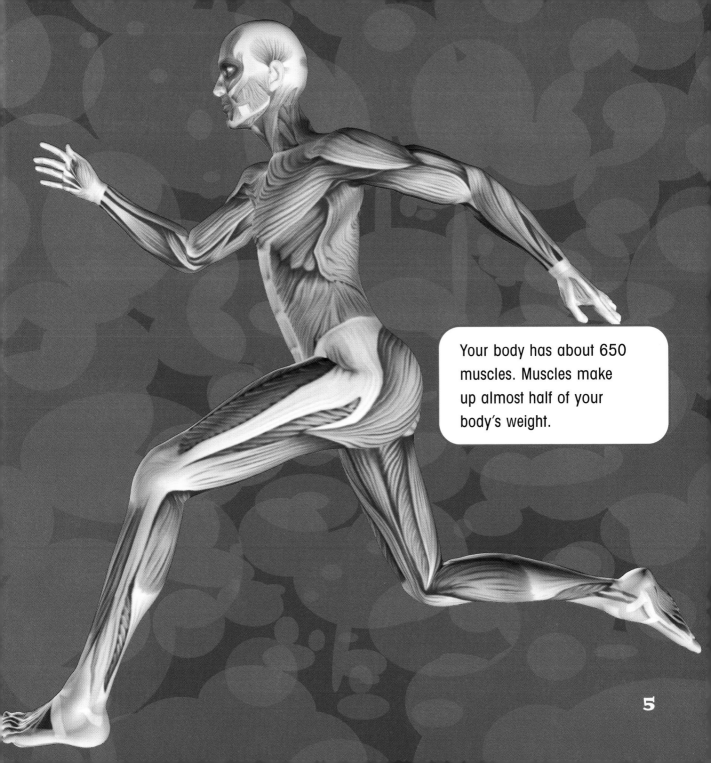

Your body has about 650 muscles. Muscles make up almost half of your body's weight.

Smooth muscles are found in the walls of the stomach. These muscles help push food from the stomach into the small intestine.
Inset: This picture shows a close-up view of cardiac muscle.

Kinds of Muscle

The three kinds of muscle in the body are called smooth muscle, **cardiac** muscle, and **skeletal** muscle. Smooth muscle is found in the walls of **organs**, such as the **small intestine**. Smooth muscles control the movement of food through the intestine.

Cardiac muscle is found only in the walls of the heart. It directs the movement of blood through the heart. Skeletal muscles are the most common kind of muscle. The body has about 400 skeletal muscles. Together with the bones, the skeletal muscles allow the body to move.

Muscles and Bones

Our skeletal muscles give us the strength to stand and walk on two feet. They also give us the power to run, to jump, and to do all the other movements we need to do.

Most skeletal muscles lie across joints. Joints are places where two or more bones meet. Each end of a muscle is fixed to the bones by strong sheets or ropes of tissue called tendons. When the muscle contracts, or presses together, it pulls on one of the bones. This causes the bone to move.

The knee is the joint that lets the leg bend. This drawing shows the muscles and tendons around the knee joint.
Inset: We would not be able to swim or surf without skeletal muscles.

People learn to make voluntary movements easily. For example, our muscles move without careful planning when we walk. *Inset:* This close-up picture shows a muscle receiving impulses from the nervous system.

Moving Muscles

Skeletal muscles are voluntary muscles. This means that you make up your mind to move them. For example, you might decide to walk across a room or raise your hand in class.

Every movement you make is controlled by the **brain** and **spinal cord**. The brain and the spinal cord make up the **central nervous system**. The central nervous system sends impulses, or messages, to the muscles. These messages cause the muscle to give off signals, or signs. These signals cause thin threads of muscle to draw close together.

Muscles Work Together

Skeletal muscles work in teams. When one group of muscles contracts, another group of muscles relaxes, or rests. To see an example of this, bend your arm at the **elbow**. The muscles on the inside of your arm contract. This pulls the bones of your lower arm toward your shoulder. Muscles in your shoulder and neck also contract to add their power to the movement. The muscles on the outside of your arm relax. Other muscles work to hold the bones of the upper arm and shoulder in place.

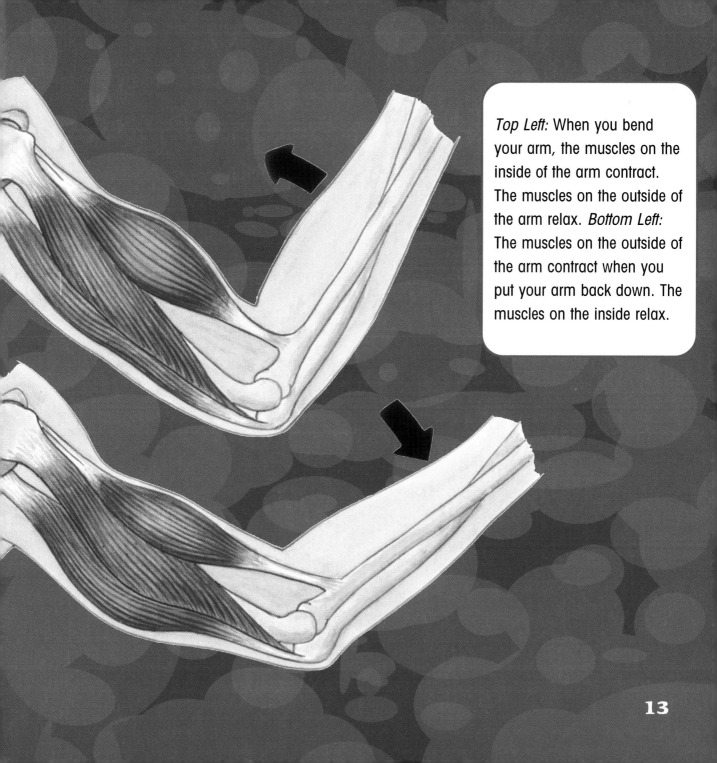

Top Left: When you bend your arm, the muscles on the inside of the arm contract. The muscles on the outside of the arm relax. *Bottom Left:* The muscles on the outside of the arm contract when you put your arm back down. The muscles on the inside relax.

This dancer is holding out her arm and her leg. These are both examples of abduction. *Inset:* Turning your head to look over your shoulder is an example of rotation.

Kinds of Movement

The skeletal muscles work together to make many kinds of movements. Flexion is the movement of one bone toward another, such as bending the arm at the elbow. Extension is the movement of one bone away from another. Straightening your arm is an example of extension.

Abduction means moving a bone away from the body's center, as you do when you raise your hand. Adduction is the movement of the bone back toward the body's center. When you turn your head, the movement is called rotation.

The Head and the Trunk

The head has two kinds of muscles. The muscles for chewing are fixed to the **jaw**. The muscles of the face are fixed to the skin. When the face's muscles move, the skin that covers them moves, too. This allows people to smile and frown.

The muscles of the trunk, or the body's middle, are wide and flat. They play an important part in breathing. They allow the upper body to turn and bend at the waist, or middle. They also give strength to the movements of the arms.

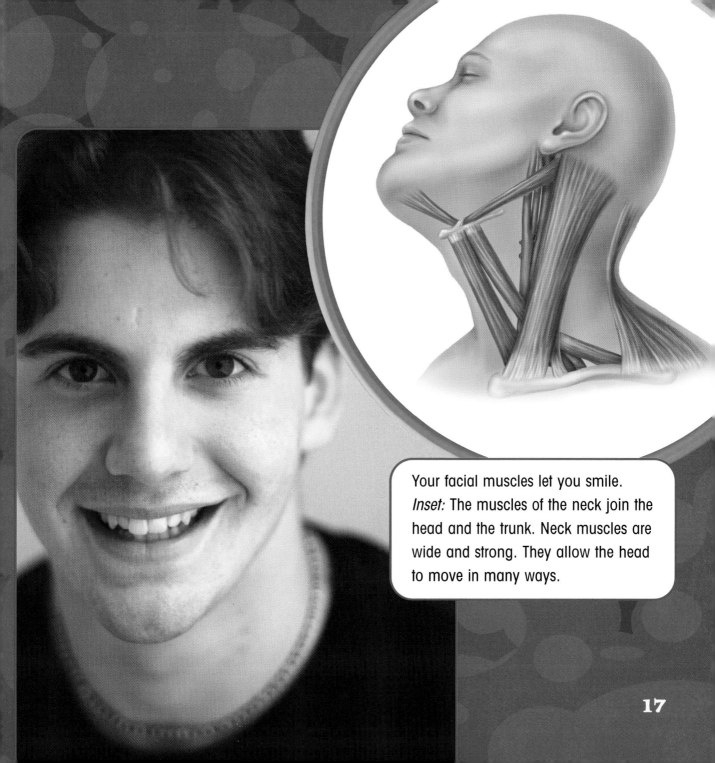

Your facial muscles let you smile.
Inset: The muscles of the neck join the head and the trunk. Neck muscles are wide and strong. They allow the head to move in many ways.

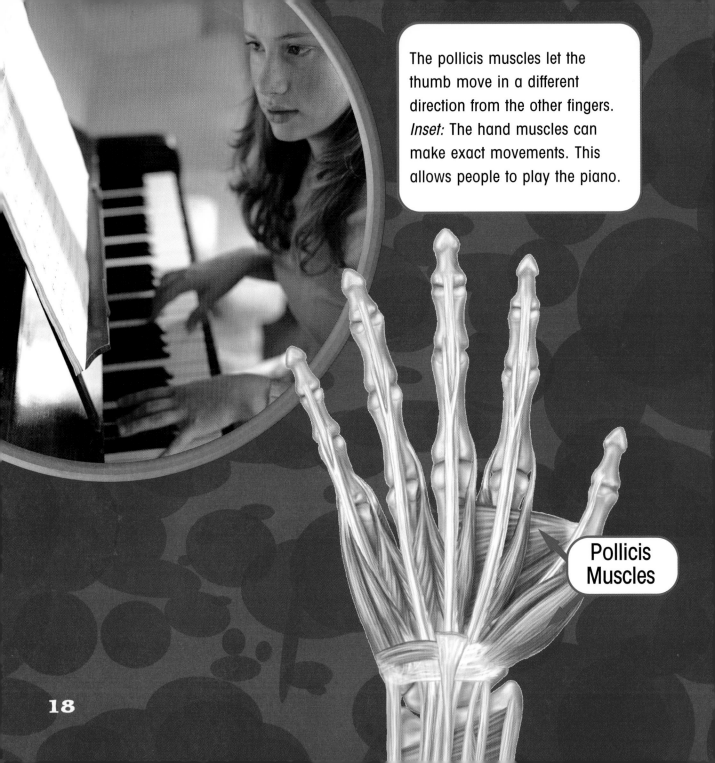

The pollicis muscles let the thumb move in a different direction from the other fingers. *Inset:* The hand muscles can make exact movements. This allows people to play the piano.

Pollicis
Muscles

The Shoulder, Arm, and Hand

The chief muscle of the shoulder is called the deltoid. It is a muscle that makes extension movements, such as raising the arm. The muscle group in the front part of the upper arm is the biceps. The group in the back is called the triceps.

The muscles of the lower arm control the movement of the hand and fingers. These muscles rotate, or turn, the hand. They also bend and straighten the fingers. The muscles of the hand are short. They are not as strong as the muscles of the arm.

The Hip, Leg, and Foot

The gluteus maximus muscles form the seat. They hold up the trunk and allow people to walk on two legs. The thigh, or upper leg, is made up of two groups of muscles called the quadriceps and the biceps. The adductor muscles reach across the inside of the thigh. They let you draw your legs together.

The most important lower leg muscles are in the back. They are tied to the heel by a sheet of tissue called the Achilles tendon. The muscles of the feet are small, but they play an important part in walking.

When the muscles of the lower leg contract, the Achilles tendon draws up the heel. When they relax, the Achilles tendon lowers the heel. *Inset:* The Achilles tendon and the muscles tied to it let you walk, run, or jump.

Achilles tendon

Heel

21

Muscular Problems

Some muscular problems can hurt the body badly. For example, Lou Gehrig's disease is an illness. It hurts the nervous system and makes it hard to send messages to the muscles. This makes the muscles powerless.

Small muscular problems are common. Your muscles may hurt during or after exercise. This pain generally goes away within a day or two. To guard the health of your muscles, exercise several times each week. Also remember to warm up before exercising. Eating well and getting enough rest will help keep your muscles healthy, too.

Glossary

brain (BRAYN) The soft body part found in the head that allows thought, movement, and feeling.

cardiac (KAR-dee-ak) Having to do with the heart.

central nervous system (SEN-trul NUR-vus SIS-tem) The brain and the spinal cord.

circulatory system (SER-kyuh-luh-tor-ee SIS-tem) The path by which blood travels through the body.

digestive system (dy-JES-tiv SIS-tem) The body parts that help turn the food you eat into the power your body needs.

elbow (EL-boh) The body part where the upper arm meets the lower arm.

jaw (JAH) Bones in the top and bottom of the mouth.

organs (OR-genz) The parts inside the body that do a job.

skeletal (SKEH-leh-tul) Having to do with bones.

small intestine (SMOL in-TES-tun) A long tunnel of tissue where food is broken down to be taken into the blood.

spinal cord (SPY-nul KORD) A long bundle of tissue that runs down the back and that carries messages between the brain and the rest of the body.

tissues (TIH-shooz) Matter that forms the parts of living things.

Index

Web Sites

Due to the changing nature of Internet links, PowerKids Press has developed an online list of Web sites related to the subject of this book. This site is updated regularly. Please use this link to access the list:
www.powerkidslinks.com/hybw/muscular/